Fishing
Into Potato Salad
By
Othen Donald Dale
Cummings

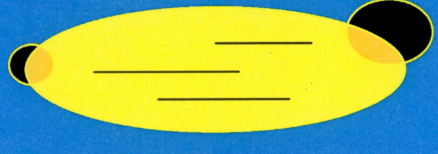

© Copyright 2014 by Othen Donald Dale Cummings. All rights reserved.
ISBN-13: 978-1501086229
ISBN-10: 1501086227

Good Morning!

I live in a small town.

I have a nice family.

The farmer likes to plow.

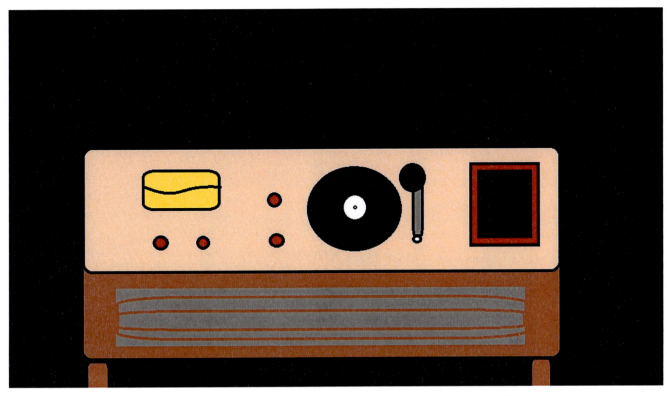

I like to listen to music.

I want a cheeseburger!

Sometimes I get angry!

Sometimes I get confused.

I like it when I'm happy!

Look at all of the monsters!

Chess is fun! I like to play chess.

A nice hot breakfast.

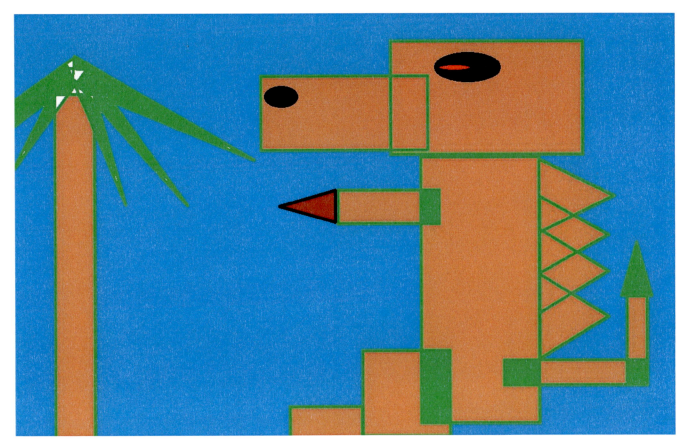

Look at the dinosaur! Is it hungry?

A pretty snowflake.

I want to ride on a train!

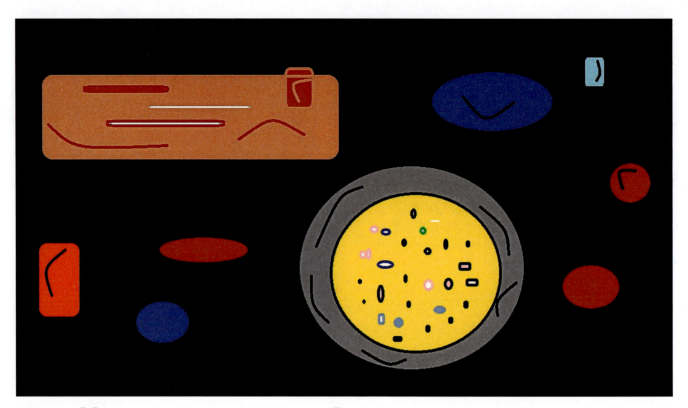

Collecting rocks is my hobby.

Sledding in the snow.

A banana split!

A white rabbit is in the magic hat!

I saw a travel trailer. It traveled down the road.

An alien planet.

A little red caboose.

Let's eat pie!

A little gray spider.

The little dog can run!

I would like a slice of hot pizza.

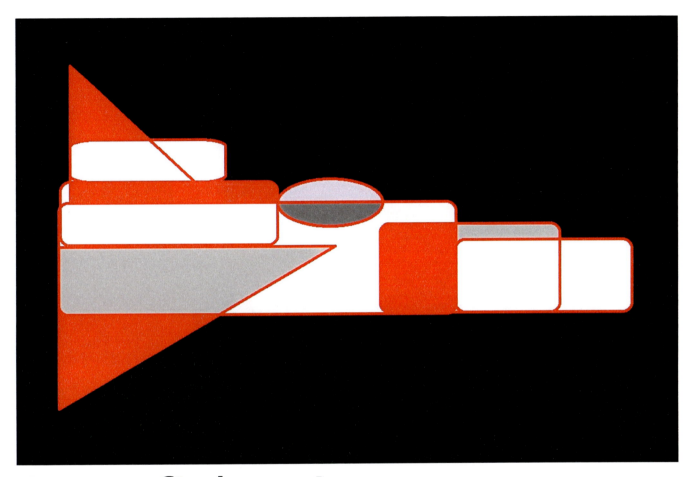

A starfighter!

Santa is on summer vacation!

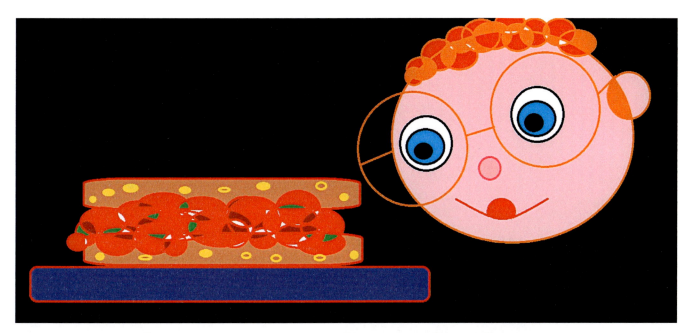

I made a sandwich for lunch.

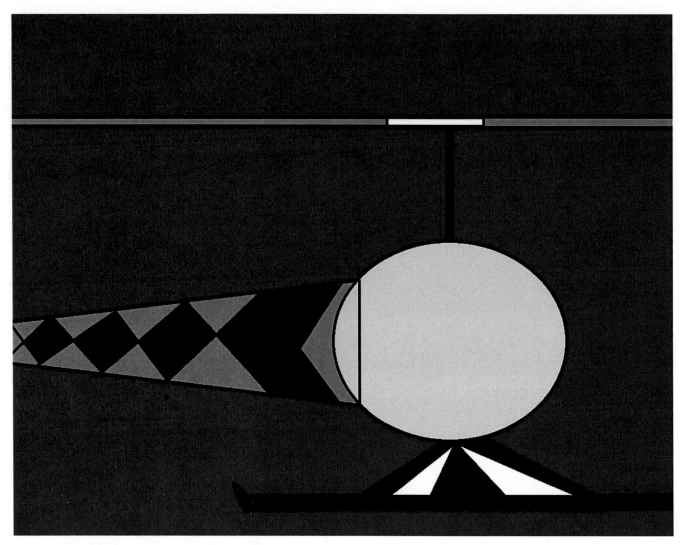

I want to fly in a helicopter.

Let's go fishing.

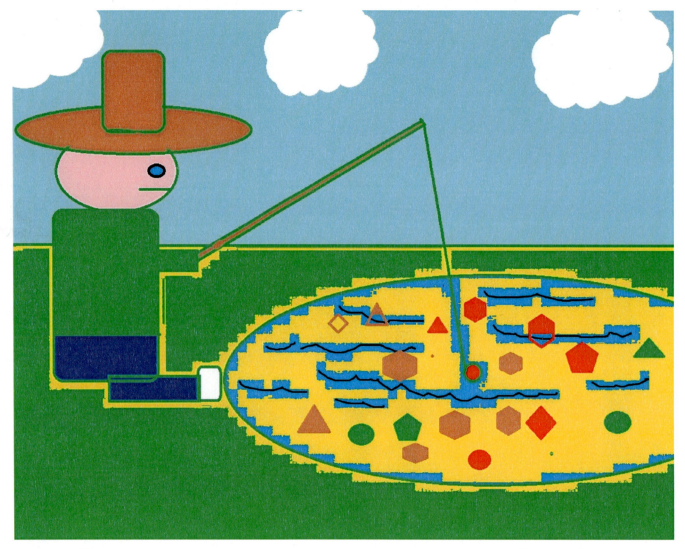

Fishing into potato salad.
It's all the rage.

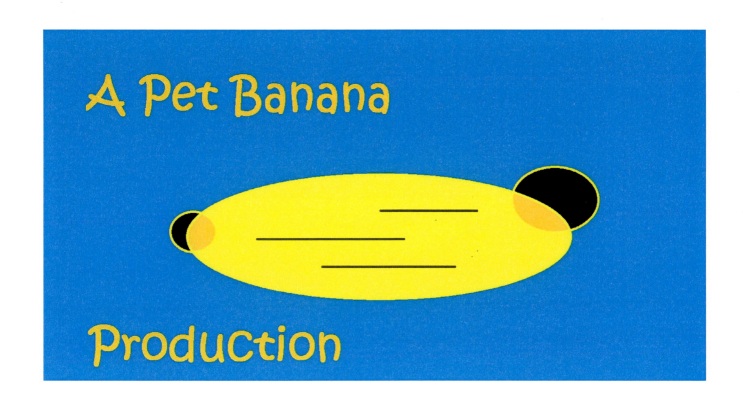

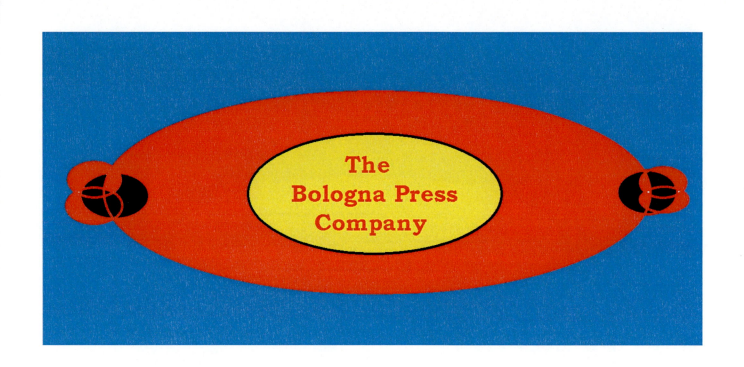

Made in the USA
San Bernardino, CA
01 August 2016